LEMON TWISTS AND TURMOIL

CANDY COVERED COZY MYSTERIES, BOOK 7

PATTI BENNING

SUMMER PRESCOTT BOOKS PUBLISHING

CHAPTER 1

THE DOOR to the candy shop was propped open, a statuette of a calico cat acting as the door stopper. Occasionally, a breeze would come through the screen door at just the right angle to blow into the shop, bringing in the fresh scents of early summer to mingle with the smells of chocolate and candy.

Candice Rothburg, the shop's owner, sat on a stool behind the counter, flipping through a magazine and looking up every couple of seconds to make sure no customers had wandered in. It was a beautiful day, and even though she would rather be out enjoying the sun than sitting in her store, and while she had been tempted to take the day off, she had refrained from it.

After all, she was about to have a whole week off. She could deal with one more day.

The door that led to the back part of the shop, which held the kitchen and the storage area, opened and Candice's best friend and half-sister, Allison, came out. The two young women were almost the spitting image of one another, and it still astounded Candice that neither of them had wondered if they were related until the truth came out. Allison's blonde hair was drawn back in a ponytail, and she was wearing a white apron, decorated with a seemingly random collection of pins and broaches. She had no idea where the other woman had found half of them. Her face was slightly flushed; the kitchen got hot in the summer, even with the big fans running.

"Twenty minutes," she said, coming to lean on the other side of the counter across from Candice. "That's how long I have to enjoy the fresh air before I have to go back and take the chocolate out of the molds."

"Should we buy another fan?" Candice asked, putting the magazine down.

"It would just blow more hot air around. We need to update the air conditioning."

Candice made a face, but she knew her friend was right. The air conditioning in the building was one of the few things that hadn't been replaced after the store burned down a couple of years ago. The unit was outside and hadn't been damaged, so even though it was old, Candice had left it as it was. Now, she was beginning to regret that.

"I'll get the pricing for a few different units and see what an install would cost. I'll try to schedule something after my trip," she said.

"Really?" Allison asked, perking up. "We'll actually have good air-conditioning this summer?"

Candice laughed. "Yeah, I promise, we won't roast all summer like we did last year."

Before Allison could reply, a customer walked into the building, glancing around curiously. Candice straightened up from her slouch and smiled brightly, one of her eyebrows raising slightly when she saw that the man was wearing a bulky jacket despite the nice weather.

"Welcome to Candice's Candies. Feel free to take a look around. Let me know if you have any questions about any of our products."

"I will, thanks," he said. "Do you own this place?"

Surprised, she nodded. "Yes, I do. Candice Rothberg."

He approached the register and shook her hand. "Jeremy Edwards. It's nice to meet you."

"I'm sorry, but how did you know I was the owner?"

"A friend of mine told me about the candy shop and mentioned you," he said. "I thought I'd stop by and check it out."

"Well, tell him thanks for me. I always appreciate news of my store spreading by word-of-mouth."

He nodded and wandered off to look at the shelves. Allison leaned a bit closer to Candice so they could talk quietly without him overhearing.

"It looks like you're getting famous," she said.

"I wish," Candice said with a chuckle. "Maybe then our online sales would go up more. No, I'm just becoming more of a name around town. It's not like with my mom, where people will come from an hour away just to check out the deli."

"Hey, locally famous counts for something," Allison said. "That's more than most people can say."

"If anything's famous, it's the candy shop, not me," she said with a snort. "I won't deny the fact the we've got the best chocolate on this side of the state."

"I'd say you're biased, but you're right. Our chocolate recipe is to die for. Hopefully, we can keep your standards up after you cruelly abandon us." Allison swooned dramatically, a betrayed expression on her face. Candice's hand twitched toward the magazine, wanting to throw it at her friend, but resisting since their customer was still nearby.

"Oh, stop it, you. It's a week. I'm sure you'll manage to hold down the fort without me."

"If this place burns down again while you're gone, remember to blame Logan and not me. You left him in charge."

"Fine. Anything terrible that happens will be his fault. That means that when I come back and see that everything ran perfectly while I was at the cottage, he'll also be the only one I give credit to." She grinned. "Maybe he'll even be the only one who gets a raise."

"Hey!"

They both started laughing until their customer approached with a pair of chocolate bars in his hand. He placed them on the counter, and Allison grinned at Candice before heading toward the kitchen, leaving her to ring up the sale.

"Did you find everything you were looking for?"

"Yes, thank you. I like the atmosphere in here. It's very… relaxed."

"Ah, yeah. Sorry, we're all kind of bummed to be stuck inside today, and I'm leaving on a trip tomorrow, so things are kind of unusual right now. We usually don't act like two crazy teens."

He chuckled. "No, don't worry. Like I said, it makes the place feel more relaxed." He reached into his jacket, then paused. "Did you say you're going on a trip? Anywhere fun?"

"Yeah, my husband and I are joining my parents on a trip up north. One of my stepdad's friends rented out a cottage for a week, but his wife broke her ankle. They decided to stay home, and he offered to let us go instead. It was kind of a last-minute thing, but it should be fun."

"That sounds nice. We used to go camping up north a lot when I was younger. Where are you going?"

"It's a tiny town called Bandon in the Upper Peninsula."

"Ah, I haven't heard of it," he said. He reached into his pants pocket and took out his wallet, putting a couple of bills down on the counter. "There you go. Have a nice trip."

"Thanks." She took the money with a smile and tucked it into the register. When she looked up, he was gone.

She was about to go back to her magazine when a beeping sound caught her attention. With a sigh, she walked over to the small taffy puller and opened the glass case. The thing had seized up again. Thankfully, this batch was only seconds away from being done, but she would have to get Logan in to look at it before tomorrow. They made all of their taffy in-store, and their new lemonade taffy was one of their most popular flavors. She had already packed away a small bag of it to bring up north; she was excited to share it with her parents. It was the perfect candy for summer, even if it was a pain to make.

Returning to the counter, she grabbed her phone and sent a text message to Logan, who was the best with their machines and appliances, then picked up her magazine. Just a few more hours, then she wouldn't have to worry about a thing for a whole week.

CHAPTER 2

CANDICE REMEMBERED TAKING family road trips when she was a child. She did not remember them being so... squished. Four adults and enough luggage for a week for each of them made even her mother's SUV feel small. They had discussed taking one of her mother's dogs earlier in their planning stages, but had quickly realized that even the smaller of the two — Maverick, the German shepherd — wouldn't have been able to fit along with their suitcases.

As Candice settled into her seat, making sure her seatbelt was pulled tight and watching the trees pass slowly by as David pulled out of the driveway, she mentally went over everything again. Her parents' dogs were safely boarding at the doggy daycare next to her mother's deli, and Candice and Eli's two cats were at their house, where Karissa, David's sister, would stop in to check on them every day. Logan was in charge of the candy shop, and she knew he would take good care of it. Eli's friend, Neil, was handling things at the dog treat bakery, along with the two other employees he had hired. Everyone who might need to reach them had their phone numbers, and in case of an emergency, they would only be four hours away.

So why did she feel so stressed? When had she reached the point where it was hard to just relax and enjoy a vacation? She took a deep breath and let it out slowly. This was supposed to be *fun*.

"Are you okay?" Eli murmured from beside her.

"Yeah. It just feels weird to be leaving."

"I know. That's probably a sign that we really need a vacation. We deserve some time to relax with the family."

She smiled and leaned into him as much as her seat-belt would allow. "Yeah, I know. I'm sorry Reggie couldn't come."

"Me too, but I don't want him to cancel his doctor's appointments for this. He understands that it was last-minute. I promised we'd go on a short trip just him and me sometime this summer."

"That will be nice for the two of you."

"Are you two plotting against us back there?" her mother asked from the front, turning around from her own whispered conversation with David.

"Definitely," Candice said.

"Well, put your plotting on hold for a second. We're trying to decide where to get lunch. Should we route to somewhere specific on our way, or do you want to just drive and stop when we come to a place that looks good in a couple of hours?"

"I'm fine with the second option," Candice said. "I like finding new places to eat, and there isn't anywhere specific I want to stop."

David and Eli gave answers to the affirmative as well, and her mother turned back to the front while David guided them out of town.

Living in the northern part of the Lower Peninsula meant that signs of civilization were sparse once they left the outskirts of town, and before long they were driving through a wilderness of trees and wetlands, with the occasional lake visible from the road. There were driveways dotted along the road, but most of them were long, the houses hidden from view by the trees. It was peaceful, and Candice felt some of the stress of her normal life already melting away.

They drove for hours, Candice reading an e-book on her phone and Eli simply leaning back and closing his eyes, while her parents talked up front about their plans for the summer. They all fell silent to look out the windows when they crossed the Mackinac Bridge, and Candice gazed out into the distance across the seemingly endless water. In some ways, the Great Lakes were such a normal part of her life that she rarely thought about them, but at times like this, when the view went on for miles, she realized how huge they truly were and felt a moment of marvel at the natural world.

Then they were past the bridge and in the Upper Peninsula, the scenery much the same as it had been but wilder and less populated. Eventually, her mother pointed out a sign in front of a tiny building that promised the best pasties in Michigan — which Candice didn't put much stock in since almost every pasty place had a similar sign — and they unanimously agreed to stop.

A few minutes later, the four of them were seated around a picnic table outside of the little restaurant, and Candice unwrapped the foil from around her pasty, biting in to taste the meat and vegetable filling. It might not have been the best pasty in Michigan, but it came close, and the taste brought back memories of other trips like this. Going up north for a summer trip and getting pasties was something Candice was sure just about every person who had grown up in Michigan could relate to.

They piled back into the car after that. Eli offered to drive, but Candice knew her mother got carsick when she sat in the back, so she wasn't surprised when the older woman declined and got behind the driver's wheel herself so David could have a break.

The rest of the trip passed quickly for Candice, since she spent her time half-dozing in the back. She didn't wake up fully until she felt the SUV slowing down, and she straightened up to see that they were pulling into a gas station in the middle of a tiny town. Her mother stopped the SUV beside a pump, then turned around in her seat.

"Good, you're awake, sleepyhead. We're in Bandon, and according to the GPS, the cottage is about ten minutes away. We're getting some gas first. Do you want to head in and grab some cold drinks or snacks?"

"Sure," Candice said. "What do you want?"

"Something fizzy. Surprise me."

Unbuckling her seatbelt, she nudged Eli, who sat up sleepily, and the two of them got out of the vehicle, heading toward the small general store that was attached to the gas station while David started pumping the gas.

The interior of the store was crowded with what looked like an entire supermarket's variety of products shoved into a space smaller than the candy shop's sales floor. The old, wooden floors were worn smooth, and some of the shelves were alarmingly crooked. Their search for cold drinks led them to the very back of the store, where a pair of old refrigerated cases hummed.

Candice grabbed a couple of sodas, figuring that whatever they didn't drink now would be welcome later that night or in the morning. They had a small cooler packed with hot dogs, condiments, and a few snacks, but hadn't brought much in the way of drinks besides coffee — an essential for all of them.

She waited while Eli picked out his own drink, then returned to the front of the store to ring up their order. The woman behind the counter was middle-aged, with the lined skin of someone who spent too much time in the sun without protection. She gave them a welcoming smile as they put their haul of drinks down.

"You headed up to camp?" she asked as she began manually entering their purchases into the register.

"We're actually renting a cottage," Candice said.

"Ah, one of Gus's?"

"I'm actually not sure, my stepdad handled the arrangements."

The woman laughed. "Trust me, if you're renting a cottage, it's one of Gus's. I swear, that man is probably responsible for a good half of all of our tourist business. There's maybe three rental properties in the whole town that aren't one of his, and none of them's nice enough to call a cottage, or big enough to hold four people. How long are you up for?"

"A week," Eli chimed in from beside her. "I'm sorry, but how did you know we were from out of town?"

The woman raised an eyebrow. "I know the locals, hun. You're not one of ours. We're a small community."

"We come from a small town too, but I don't think even my grandfather knows everyone."

"There's small towns, and then there's small towns." She chuckled. "I'm Eden Copeland. You can go ahead and call me Eden. If you're staying for a week, I'm sure we'll see plenty of each other. Don't hesitate to swing by if you need directions or recommendations of places to visit."

"It's nice to meet you," Candice said. "I'm Candice, and this is Eli. We're here with my parents, David and Moira."

"David's the tall one, with dark hair and a green shirt?"

Surprised, Candice nodded. Eden glanced out the glass door. "It looks like he's found a twin. Is he an evil mastermind, by chance? Or part of a soap opera?"

Candice and Eli both leaned slightly to see what she was looking at, and sure enough, David was talking with another man almost exactly the same height with dark hair and wearing almost the exact same color shirt.

"No, but he's a private investigator," Candice said, amused.

"Darn, I don't think those are prone to having evil twins. Would you like a bag?"

Candice forced her attention back to the other woman to accept the plastic bag and hand over what she owed for the sodas. Eden put a register closed sign on the counter and slipped outdoors, shooting an amused look at the two men before going around to the back of the building. Candice and Eli followed, heading for David and his twin.

Her stepfather glanced over as they approached and waved her and Eli closer. He was grinning, and the man he was talking to looked equally amused. Up close, their features were obviously different, but from a distance or from behind, they looked quite similar. Both were tall, dark-haired, and were wearing jeans and a green shirt, though David's buttoned up.

"Candice, Eli, this is Frank. My long-lost twin brother."

Candice looked between them. "Seriously?"

Frank burst out laughing. "No, but you'd almost believe it, wouldn't you? I was just minding my own business, throwing away some fast food wrappers, when this man's wife comes up and touches my arm, telling me she's going to head to the restroom. You should have seen her face when I turned around."

David chuckled. "I was watching. I've never seen Moira look so surprised."

"David came over and introduced himself and we had a good laugh. Would one of you mind taking a picture of us? I want to send it to my kids. I'm going to try that twin line. I want to see how long I can keep them wondering."

"Sure," Candice said. She handed Eli the bag with the sodas and took her cell phone out of her back pocket. Frank flopped an arm around David's shoulders and they both grinned. She snapped a couple of pictures for good measure.

"Thanks. I'll give you my number, if you can send them. This was a great way to liven up my trip."

While Eli walked back to the SUV to deposit the heavy bag, Candice sent Frank the photos, then shook his hand. "It was nice to meet you. I'll be sure to joke with my mom about it later."

"I think I almost gave the poor woman a heart attack." Still chuckling, he turned to shake David's hand. "It was great to run into you. Have a good vacation, man."

"You too," David said.

Frank nodded to them both, then headed around to the back of the building, where the restroom sign was pointing. Candice chuckled as she turned to head toward the SUV, imagining her mother's surprise. She wondered if she'd run in to the man again on her way out of the restroom, which was good for another chuckle. She knew her mother was a good sport and would laugh along with their joking. As far as she was concerned, this was a great way to start their vacation.

She had almost reached the car, with David right behind her, when a scream pierced the air. She jumped and spun around, her eyes searching for the noise. In just seconds, she realized there was only one place it could have come from; behind the gas station, where the restrooms were.

CHAPTER 3

CANDICE AND DAVID rushed toward the back of the building, Eli close behind them. As she ran, a million thoughts rushed through Candice's mind, all about her mother. Had she been hurt? Attacked? Or had Frank just surprised her again? She wanted to believe the last one, but she knew her mother didn't scare that easily. She wouldn't scream over a jump scare, not like that.

When she rounded the corner, she skidded to a halt, stopping so quickly she almost fell over when she saw the blood. Her heart was in her throat and she didn't know if she was brave enough to lift her eyes to the body she could see lying on the ground in her peripheral vision.

"Moira!" David called out, hurrying forward and drawing her mother into his arms. Her shaken, but living and breathing mother, who appeared unharmed.

Almost dizzy from relief, Candice finally focused on the body. When she saw the dark hair and green shirt, she took a reflexive step back, bumping into Eli, who wrapped his arms around her.

"Frank," she said. Behind her, she heard the sound of the other bathroom door opening. She glanced around in time to see Eden come out. The woman pressed her hands to her mouth, a horrified expression on her face at the sight of the body.

"What happened?" David asked.

He was reaching into his pocket as he spoke and pulled out his phone, frowning as he stared at the screen and then lifted it higher, moving it around as if he was searching for a signal. Remembering that she'd had enough of a signal to send the photos to Frank, she reached into her pocket for her own phone, listening as her mother spoke.

"I was washing my hands when I heard something," she said. "There was a shout, then a voice saying something, but I couldn't make it out. I thought maybe one of you was looking for me, so I came out and I almost tripped over him."

She glanced at the body, then looked away again quickly. David released her long enough to crouch down and check for a pulse, only to shake his head and stand back up. Candice was not surprised - it looked like he had been stabbed right through the heart.

With a jolt, she remembered why she had taken her phone out and dialed 911, raising the phone to her ear in time to catch the dispatcher's greeting. Taking a deep breath, she tried to focus enough to explain what had happened.

Candice had thought Lake Marion was bad about attracting crowds when there was an emergency, but Bandon had it beat by miles. Before the emergency services even arrived, a crowd had gathered, and it seemed to be growing every second. Eden was standing at the edge of the crowd, talking into a cell phone, and a couple from the house whose yard bordered the back parking lot had dragged chairs over to watch the proceedings. Occasionally a newcomer called out, asking who it was, and every time someone answered that it was an out-of-towner, a collective relief seemed to go through the group.

She didn't miss the glances that were sent their way either, nor the whispers that followed them. They were out-of-towners. Strangers. And they had been the ones to find the body.

Her discomfort grew steadily until an ancient police cruiser pulled into the back lot, driving slowly as the crowd of people separated. She could hear sirens drawing closer — probably the ambulance. Idly, she wondered how far away the closest hospital was. It had to be at least a good twenty minutes by ambulance, if not further.

"All right, everyone, get back," the officer said as he stepped out of his vehicle. He approached the body slowly, crouching down to check the man's vitals, and then unclasped an antique looking radio from his belt and reported codes to dispatch. He looked up, his eyes landing on Candice and her family immediately.

"Are you the ones who found him?"

"Yes," David said, his arm still around Moira.

"You four, stay. I need everyone else to clear out. This is a crime scene. Don't make me charge anyone for loitering."

With a grumble, the crowd began to disperse, but Eden hesitated. "Mark, I was in the second stall when I heard someone scream. Do you want me to stick around? I'm happy to give a statement."

The officer shook his head. "You can get back to manning the store, Eden. I'll come around front when I'm ready to talk to you. Unless you've got an idea of who did this?"

She shook her head. "No, sir, I haven't the faintest." Candice thought she saw the woman's eyes dart toward David, but all she said after her pause was, "I'll be waiting around front, then. There'll be a cold one in the fridge with your name on it when you stop in."

She walked away, and the officer, Mark, continued looking over the body, frowning. He didn't say anything else until the ambulance arrived, when he made room for the paramedics to declare death.

While they worked, he approached Candice and the

others. He looked grim, but seemed friendly enough when he introduced himself as Officer Mark Hotch.

"Thanks for waiting," he said. "Why don't you tell me what happened?"

They told their story, David starting with meeting Frank, and Moira finishing with hearing the shout outside the bathroom. The officer asked them a handful of basic questions, like if they had seen anyone else go around to the back of the building, and whether Frank seemed nervous at all. At last, he looked up from his notepad with a sigh.

"Are you folks going to be around town for a while?"

Candice saw her mother and stepfather exchange a look, then David glanced over to her and Eli. "We were planning on staying for a week, but I don't know if we're still in the mood for a vacation. What do you think?"

Officer Hotch spoke when Candice hesitated. "It might help our investigation. There's a possibility that we will need to speak with one or all of you again, or ask you to come in to look at a lineup."

"We can stay," Candice said, after a quick glance at

Eli to make sure he didn't object. "I think we'd all like to help, if we can."

Officer Hotch nodded and took down their address and contact information before telling them they were free to go. As they walked away, Candice glanced back and saw him frowning down at Frank's body.

"Well, today could have gone better," David said as they all got back in the SUV.

"He looked so much like you," Moira said, looking at her husband with an unidentifiable expression on her face. "So much, David. I thought it was you at first."

He grabbed her hand and squeezed for a moment, then let it go to put his seatbelt on. "Let's head out. We still need to pick up the key for the cottage, then I'm going to have to take a drive around to see if I can find a spot with cell service. If not, I may have to borrow your cell phone, Candice. I'm helping Lenny with a case, and I was expecting a call from him to go over some stuff. Last I heard, our client was missing. Which isn't a great sign, since he hired us for a missing person's case in the first place. I'm worried, and I want to make sure he's contacted Lenny."

"Of course," Candice said. Usually she would have

made a joke about how he should have switched to the carrier that she and Eli had, but the words died on her tongue. None of them were in a joking mood anymore.

CHAPTER 4

IT TOOK ONLY another couple of minutes of driving before they were pulling down a long dirt road. A handful of driveways branched off, but when David turned down the last one, they ended up in front of a small, white, wooden cottage with a number five on the door. No other houses were visible. All Candice could see were trees and, about a hundred feet away from the cottage's front door, the lake. There was a small dock with a boat tethered to it, and a big, blue SUV was parked by the edge of the water.

"This is it," David said unnecessarily as he put their vehicle into park. They all got out, and Candice breathed in the fresh air. It was beautiful, but it was hard to fully enjoy it after seeing what they had just come from.

"Hey, there," a man's voice called out. He came around from the other side of the blue SUV and waved at them. "Are you David?"

"I am," David said, stepping forward to shake the man's hand. "I'm David and this is Moira, and my stepdaughter Candice and her husband, Eli."

"I'm Angus Fowler, but everyone calls me Gus. I'm glad you were able to take over the rental on such short notice. I've got the keys right here, I'll just need you to sign for them first. Boat's good to go, though you'll want to get more gas for her. There's a gas cannister in the shed. The rules are simple; only light fires in the wood burning stove inside or the firepit outside. No smoking indoors, and clean up your mess when you're done. Anything gets broken or lost, and you're responsible for it. I know it looks pretty isolated, but sound travels over the water and you've got some neighbors on either side, so no loud music or shouting after eleven or so. If you clean fish, I'd appreciate it if you do it outside. There's a washbasin and worktable out behind the house for that purpose. You can just throw the guts back in the lake."

"Thanks," David said. "We shouldn't have any trouble with any of that. It all sounds like common sense."

Gus opened the door to his SUV and took out a clipboard and a pen, chuckling. "Well, you'd be surprised how many people don't have a lick of common sense. Most people are pretty polite, but occasionally we'll get guests who leave the place a mess. I've found it's best to get everything in writing, so there's no confusion. Now, you're the only one who needs to sign, since your name's on the agreement. I've only got the two keys, so you'll have to make that work between the four of you."

"Not a problem," David said as he signed. Gus handed over the keys and shook his hand. He turned to put the clipboard back in the car, and Candice took a few steps toward the cottage, eager to check out the inside.

A branch rustled to her left, and she turned just as a hunched over man burst out of what looked like a game trail through the forest. He was clutching an axe, and Candice stumbled back with a shriek.

The man stopped, and Candice felt Eli come up

behind her. "Sorry, sorry, didn't mean to scare yeh," the man said.

"Oh, this is Alfie," Gus said from behind her. "He's the groundskeeper for a few of my properties. He lives just down that path there, so if you folks need anything, don't hesitate to go find him. How's it going, Alfie?"

"I just got finished chopping firewood for Cottage Four," he said. "I came over to see if these folks needed any more before I head into town."

"I think they're good; the previous guests didn't use any."

"All right." Alfie turned to David and Moira. "If you run out, go ahead and knock on my door. If I'm not in, just drop a note in the box on the table by the door, and I'll come chop some more when I see it."

"Thank you," David said. "You've both been very helpful."

"We'll leave you to get settled in," Gus said. "See you tonight, Alfie?"

"Same as usual, boss."

Gus got into his SUV and started it, pulling out of the driveway with a wave. From behind them, Alfie said, "Well, if you're sure you don't need anything, I'm going to head to the next cottage. Firewood doesn't chop itself."

"Thank you," David said. "I don't think we need anything right now, but we'll come find you if we do."

They waited while Alfie walked down another slender path through the trees before disappearing into the shadows. Candice sighed and leaned back against the car.

"Right. Guy with an axe. I didn't see that coming."

"He seemed nice," Eli said. "Come on, let's go check out the cottage."

They got a key from David, who seemed more interested in going down to the dock to examine the boat, and made their way to the cottage. Eli pulled open the screen door with a loud creak, and unlocked the main door, pushing it open and then moving aside for Candice.

She stepped inside, looking around with a smile. It

was quaint, which was to be expected. There was a faint musty smell in the air; the scent of a building that spent most of its time not lived in. The entranceway opened into the kitchen, which featured an old gas stove, a small refrigerator, a microwave, and a couple of cupboards, one of which was partially open, revealing a stack of old plastic cups, turned upside down to keep the dust out.

The living room was to her left, and had a worn but comfortable looking couch, an equally worn and somewhat threadbare armchair, and a wood stove. The center of the room featured what looked like a handmade wooden coffee table, and there were stacks of board games underneath.

"It looks nice," Eli said, coming to stand beside her. "We should play Monopoly tonight."

"You do *not* want to see how competitive my mom and I get over Monopoly."

The two of them explored the rest of the cottage. There was only one bathroom, which meant that all four of them would have to share. The two bedrooms were nice; one was decorated in a floral theme, and the other in a nautical one. The nautical themed one looked out over the lake, and the other looked into the woods. The place was small, but it would more than do for their weeklong stay, especially considering that the lake was right there — and she had brought both an inflatable tube and her bathing suit. She was determined to spend some time in the water, even if it wasn't yet as warm as it would be later in the year.

She was going to have a nice vacation if it killed her.

CHAPTER 5

THEY SPENT the next few hours settling in; Moira and Candice unpacked the cooler and started making a list of what they wanted to get from town, while David took the boat out for a spin, and Eli tried to untangle the fishing poles they had found in the shed. It was starting to get dark when David came in and announced he was going into town.

"I've got to find somewhere with cell service, and I can stop and grab some food while I'm out. Do we need anything?"

"Hot dog buns," Moira said. "That's all we need for tonight. We can do a bigger trip tomorrow as a family."

"We need worms too," Eli chimed in. "I've only managed to dig up a few, and I was thinking about waking up early to fish for breakfast. I can go with you if you want."

"No, that's okay," he said. "You guys should stay here and have fun. I'll be back soon."

He kissed his wife goodbye and left, shutting the door behind him. Moira walked over to the coffee table in the living room and began looking through the board games.

"Most of these are better with more than three people," she said. "Though we could play Scrabble."

"Too much thinking," Candice said. "I know we didn't do all that much today, but I'm tired. Traveling always makes me exhausted."

"Why don't you and Eli get a fire going in the fire pit outside? That way when David returns with the buns, we can get started on the hot dogs?"

That sounded good to Candice. She and Eli put their shoes on and grabbed a lighter and an old newspaper from the kitchen, then went outside. She grabbed two of the camp chairs they had brought with them from the porch and set them up while Eli fetched a few pieces of wood from the shed.

"We're going to need to look for smaller sticks to get it going," he said as he dumped the logs next to the fire pit.

"Right. Whoever gets the most has to make a hot dog for the other person?"

"You're on," he replied with a grin.

Turning her phone's flashlight on, Candice headed for the thicker part of the woods while Eli went toward the trees by the lake. She kept her eyes on the ground, looking for small, dry sticks that would make good kindling for the fire. She wanted to win, more because she enjoyed winning than because of the few minutes it would take to make a hot dog.

She bent down to gather a few sticks, discarding one that had turned mushy with decomposition, then straightened up suddenly. Had that been a stick snapping off to her right?

Frozen, she listened in silence for a moment, but

didn't hear anything else. She continued picking up sticks for a few more seconds before the sound of breaking sticks and crunching leaves made her freeze again, her heart pounding. There was definitely something big out there. She knew that Michigan's Upper Peninsula had both black bears and wolves. As far as she knew, wolves almost never attacked humans, and black bears usually didn't, unless they had cubs or were used to associating humans with food.

Neither of those facts felt particularly helpful just then, given that she didn't have the faintest idea when black bear breeding season was, and she had no doubt that the bears in such a touristy area would be used to stealing food from garbage cans and unattended picnic tables.

Trying not to make noise, she began backing toward the tree line, using her phone's ineffectual flashlight to try to look into the darkness. She couldn't see anything, but whatever was out there was still moving around. When she reached the edge of the trees, she turned and ran back toward the fire pit, dumping her handful of sticks next to it. A second light showed Eli's approach, and he released a much larger pile of sticks.

"Did you give up?" he asked.

"There's something out there," she replied, shaken. "I heard it moving around in the woods."

"It's probably just a deer or something," he said. "Do you want to go look?"

"Not really, but we probably should." She sighed, then reached over and took his hand. "Stick close. I don't want to be alone out there."

"Don't worry. I'm not going anywhere."

They returned to the spot where she had been looking for sticks, both of their phones lit. Eli looked around and after listening for a moment, he shrugged. "I don't hear anything. Like I said, it was probably a deer. You must have scared it away."

"I hope so."

The cottage's screen door creaked loudly enough that they could hear it even from the woods. "Candice? Eli?"

"We're coming, Mom," Candice shouted back. She tugged Eli back to the tree line, then let go of his hand

and put her phone in her pocket as she approached her mother, trying to shake off the feeling that something was still out there. "What is it?"

"I just wanted to know what you wanted?"

"What we wanted?"

Her mother gave her a puzzled frown. "Weren't you knocking?"

"No. What do you mean? We were in the woods."

"I thought I heard someone knocking." The older woman ran a hand down her face. "I must be getting tired. How's the fire coming?"

"We haven't started it yet," Candice said, only half paying attention. She was too busy looking around and beside her. Eli was doing the same.

"I'll come out and help you. David should be back soon."

"No... No, it's okay. We've got it."

Her mother gave her a slightly concerned look, but nodded and let the door swing shut. Candice gestured with her head, and Eli followed her over to the fire pit. She picked up the lighter and a page of the newspaper, and began building a pile of kindling with some of the small sticks. She spoke in a lowered voice while she fiddled with it.

"Eli, I swear I heard something out there. And then with my mom hearing a knock… do you think there's someone out here with us?"

"I don't think so," he said. "I think you're just…"

"Just what?" she asked. "Hearing things? Being para-noid?" She fell silent when she realized his eyes were looking at something over her left shoulder. She turned around slowly, feeling as though the pit of her stomach was filled with ice. Her eyes landed on a shadowy figure by the trees and she fell backward with a scream, slamming her elbow against the fire pit.

"I'm sorry! I keep doing that to yeh, don't I?" a vaguely familiar voice said. Eli turned on his phone's light and it lit up the face of the groundskeeper, Alfie.

"You scared me to death!" Candice snapped, letting Eli help her up. "Was that you sneaking around in the woods earlier? Did you knock on the cottage's door?"

PATTI BENNING

"No, I didn't. Have you seen someone else sneaking around?"

"Not seen," Eli said. "But Candice and her mother both heard someone. What are you doing here?"

"I got a complaint from another cottage that a man was looking in their windows. By the time I got there, he was gone. I figured I might as well check on you, since yours was the next down the line. No one's hurt or anything?"

"Just my elbow," Candice said, rubbing it.

"Any chance you could give me a description of him?"

"Like Eli said, we never actually saw anyone."

There was the sound of tires on gravel, and a pair of headlights spilled down the driveway. Candice felt a sense of relief. "That'll be my stepdad."

"If there was someone here, I doubt he'll be coming back," Alfie said. "Let me know if there are any other issues, okay?"

"We will," Eli said as Alfie walked away. By the time

44

David got out of the SUV, he had vanished into the trees again.

"Who was that?" he asked. Candice heard a beep as he locked the car and saw a shopping bag hanging in his hand as he approached them.

"The groundskeeper," she said with a sigh. "It's been a weird half-hour."

CHAPTER 6

CANDICE WAS on edge while they all sat around the fire and roasted their hot dogs, but nothing else creepy, or even mildly unsettling, happened that night. She and Eli got a restful night's sleep in the nautical themed bedroom and were up early — Eli to fish and Candice to sit on the couch and drink coffee while she stared hazily at her phone.

"Hey, David, did you ever make that call you needed to make last night?" she asked when he walked through to the kitchen. He idly grabbed one of the lemonade taffies she had brought from the bag on the counter.

"No. I never did find a spot that had service, and by the time I got back, I thought it was late enough that I might as well just call in the morning. Are you still okay with me using your phone?"

"I would be, but I don't have any service out here either. We'll have to go back into town for it."

"Did you mention going into town for something?" her mother asked, coming out of the bedroom. "I have a list of what we need."

"We can all go," Candice said. "We didn't really get a chance to look around yesterday."

The door opened and Eli came in, making a beeline over to the sink to wash his hands. He patted them dry with a hand towel, then poured himself a cup of coffee.

"Any luck?" Candice asked.

"Nothing big enough to keep."

"Well, we were just talking about going to town. We can get breakfast there."

The little town looked peaceful and calm when they drove into it a short while later. It was hard to imagine that a man had been killed there the day before, but as they drove by the combination gas station and general store, Candice couldn't seem to keep her eyes off the parking lot. When she wasn't actively trying not to think about Frank, her heart ached for him. He had seemed so happy, and when she had taken that picture of him and David, he'd had no idea that his life could be measured in minutes instead of decades.

She forced herself to turn from the window as they drove by and realized that David was speaking. "...it when I came to town last night. What do you think?"

"Sure," Moira said. "Anything sounds good to me right now."

Eli also answered in the affirmative, and so did Candice, guessing that they were talking about a place to get breakfast. Her guess turned out to be correct; they pulled into the parking lot of a small building whose sign held a picture of a mouthwatering plate of eggs, hash browns, and bacon. Another sign on the front door read *Breakfast All Day!*

The interior of the restaurant was homey and surprisingly busy for such a small town. About a third of the tables were full, and there were sounds of steady work coming from the kitchen. A waitress who was behind the register, checking a guest out, waved at them and said, "Go ahead and sit anywhere. I'll be with you in just a second."

They seated themselves at a free table and looked at the menu, which was all breakfast items. If the pictures were anything to go by, the portions they served were huge. *Maybe I'll take some home for later,* she thought. It wasn't long before the waitress came by and they placed their drink orders, and she then returned to ask after their food choices.

Candice sipped her orange juice while she waited for the food to come out. None of the four of them seemed to be in a particularly talkative mood; the smells in the diner did nothing but remind Candice how hungry she was, especially after a meal the night before that consisted solely of hot dogs.

It wasn't long before the waitress came back, carrying two trays loaded with plates that were piled sky-high with food. She set Candice's eggs, hash browns, and bacon in front of her, and a plate with a tower of pancakes on it in front of Eli, along with a smaller plate that held only bacon. Her parents received similar plates, and her mother looked at hers in surprise.

"I had no idea there would be so much," she said as the waitress walked away. "I'm never going to finish all of this."

"We'll have leftovers," David said, digging in. "That's only ever a good thing."

Candice grabbed the bottle of hot sauce from the basket of condiments by the wall and shook some out onto her hash browns before starting to work on her own food. It was good — greasy and salty and nothing she would be able to eat every day, but perfect vacation food. After a quick, whispered conversation bartering with Eli, she traded him one of her eggs for one of his pancakes, then stole a sip of the overly sweetened coffee he had gotten.

A good third of her food was left by the time she felt too full to continue, but the waitress was more than happy to supply them with boxes. They left her a good tip and returned to the SUV in silence, this time because they were all too full to want to talk much.

"What does everyone want to do now?" David asked as Candice put her box in the back of the vehicle.

"Well, we still have to get groceries," Moira said.

"I wanted to walk around town a bit, but I think I'm too full for that right now," Candice said. "We could go get groceries, head back to the cottage and drop off the food, and then maybe go out again."

It was a plan, though not as simple as it had seemed at first. They all piled into the SUV, ready to head toward the grocery store, when they realized none of them actually knew where the store was. Bandon was a tiny town, not much more than the buildings that lined the streets that intersected at the main intersection and a scattering of private residences and tourist accommodations surrounding it, which meant that there weren't many places for a grocery store to be hiding. At last, after even Candice's phone failed to connect to the GPS long enough to tell them where to go, her mother hopped out and went into the restaurant they had just left. She came back a moment later and directed David to drive toward the combined gas station and general store in the middle of town.

"It turns out that place is what passes as their grocery store," Moira said. "And their hardware store and feed store."

"Well, that explains why Eden was so certain she'd be seeing us again," Candice said. "Though after what happened last time we went there, I don't know how friendly she'll be."

David parked in front of the store, joining the other three vehicles that were there, and the four of them got out and made their way into the store. Eden was behind the counter with another customer, but she gave them a smile and a wave when she saw them. Candice relaxed slightly. It seemed that the other woman had no hard feelings.

"I'll be right back," David said, striding down an aisle and out of sight.

"Okay," Moira said slowly, staring after him. "What got into him?" She shook her head. "Well, we might as well split up and grab what we need. The car's unlocked, so we can just meet up there when we're done."

Eli and Candice walked around the cluttered store, grabbing what they deemed as necessities for the next few days. The store seemed to have no real sense of organization. Aisles were either food or non-food, but other than that, it was chaos. They finally found the refrigerated section through a door at the back of the store, which she hadn't even noticed last time.

When they left the chilly, refrigerated room, they almost ran into David and another man he seemed to be in deep discussion with, who Candice recognized as Gus, the man whose cottage they were renting.

She couldn't catch their words, but whatever they were talking about, it ended on a handshake. Something about it seemed tense to her, but before she could decide what it was exactly, David turned to her and smiled. "About done?"

"Yeah, I think we have everything," she said. "We'll meet you at the car."

She and Eli exchanged *what was that about* looks, but didn't say anything as they returned to the front of the store and piled their goods on the counter. Eden beamed at them.

"I'm glad to see you two back. I was worried we'd scared you away. How do you like the cottage?"

"It's lovely," Candice said. "It's nice, being right next to the lake. I could get used to that."

"You'd love everything but the taxes," the older woman said with a chuckle as she rang the items up. "So, you're staying for your full week?"

"That's the plan."

"Well, then you've absolutely got to come in here on Friday. My daughter makes homemade pies to sell, and they're best fresh."

"We'll definitely keep that in mind," Candice said, beginning to gather up the bags while Eli paid. "Thanks for the recommendation. I'm sure we'll be in again before we leave."

CHAPTER 7

"WHAT WAS THAT ABOUT?" Candice asked David once they had all piled into the SUV.

"You mean what I was talking about with Gus?" he asked. She nodded. "I was just asking him about that groundskeeper. I don't like that he was snooping around last night."

"He said he was following another person," Candice said.

"Did you see anyone other than him?" he asked. Frowning, she shook her head. It hadn't seemed to her that Alfie was lying, but she supposed he could be. She guessed it made sense David just wanted to double check on him, since he had been sneaking around their cottage late at night.

They put their food away when they returned, then Candice joined Eli on the dock while he fished. He caught a few small bluegill, but nothing worth keeping, and let them go in the lake. She was leaning against a post, reading one of the books she had brought with her. It was relaxing, but it was also strange not to feel as though there was something else she was supposed to be doing. She checked her phone periodically- a bad habit - but while she had service in town, there was no such luck out here.

She hadn't called to check in with the store while she was in town, and while part of her regretted it, the other part was proud. She had only been gone for a day, after all. What could really have gone wrong in that time?

The screen door opened, and she turned to see David and her mother coming out of the cottage. David was carrying a tackle box, and her mother carried an inflatable inner tube. Both had towels draped over their arms, and David was also pulling a cooler behind him.

"We're going to head out on the boat," David said when he saw them. "Do you want to come with us?"

She and Eli only had to trade a glance before they agreed; he'd be able to continue fishing out there, and she'd be able to keep reading, but with the added benefit of enjoying the fresh breeze while they were boating. It didn't take them long to grab what they wanted, and for Candice to change into her bathing suit. The boat was small, but large enough to fit all four of them comfortably, and she took one of the seats, reaching over to help him untie a rope after David started the motor.

"While I was talking to Gus, he gave me a couple of locations that are known for having good fishing," he said. "I thought we could check those out."

Candice wasn't big on fishing herself – she did it occasionally, but preferred to spend her time in the water, rather than catching fish out of it – but she knew it was something the guys enjoyed, so she didn't mind. Besides, fresh fish for lunch would be good.

She settled back into her seat as David guided them around the dock and toward the west side of the lake. Once they got away from the shore, he sped up, and

Candice closed her eyes against the wind. It was an almost perfect day for this; sunny and warm, but with a breeze that kept them cool. There were clouds dotted here and there in the sky, but no threat of rain. She trailed her hand in the water. It was cool, but not cold. If she got too warm from the sun, she could always jump in for a quick cool down.

David pulled the boat close to the shore, keeping them in the sun but close enough to the dappled shade under the trees that they could cast their lines into it. While he and Eli prepared the hooks, Candice's mother laid out a pair of towels. Candice joined her, sliding on her sunglasses and laying back in the sunlight, chatting with her mother for a bit about how their trip was going so far, while she put sunscreen on before letting the warmth and the gentle rocking of the ship – and occasional splashes when one of the guys caught something – lull her into a doze.

A big splash and excited voices woke her, and she propped herself up on her elbows to see David lean over the side of the boat to net a fish Eli had caught. She and her mother scrambled back a moment later when the fish jumped out of the net and began flip flopping across the boat.

Eli dove on top of it and, after a moment's wrestling, held the fish down long enough for David to measure it.

"Yes!" Eli exclaimed. David quickly filled a bucket with water, and Eli slipped the fish inside. "Finally got one big enough to keep," he explained when he noticed his wife and mother-in-law watching in amusement.

"Good," Moira said. "I'm starting to get hungry."

They headed back toward the cottage after a short discussion about whether they wanted to bother blowing up the inner tube and take turns getting towed back. Since they had the rest of the vacation in front of them and no one wanted to spend the time blowing the thing up, they decided to wait. The promise of lunch was making Candice's stomach begin to growl, though breakfast had only been a few hours ago. It was around when she normally took her lunch break at work, so she supposed it made sense. Her body had grown used to her schedule; hopefully it would pick it up again without trouble once she got back home.

David slowed the boat down as they drew near a spot

of shoreline that looked familiar. Candice had the feeling that if it was up to her alone, she wouldn't have recognized their dock, but her stepfather seemed to know where to go.

Or so she thought. "Hey, I think this is the wrong dock," she said as they drew near to it. "We must be the next one down."

"No, that's our SUV," David said. "Why?"

"I swear I saw someone walk past the kitchen window."

Frowning, David cut the engine and let the boat drift in silence for a moment. All four of them stared at the cottage. Candice was beginning to wonder if she was going insane, but a minute later she saw the movement past the kitchen window again, and this time whoever it was pushed the screen door open and walked out of the house.

The person was too far away for Candice to be able to see any identifying details. Whoever it was wore a baseball cap and a dark-colored sweatshirt. It seemed a bit too warm for the sweatshirt, but then she had been lying in the sun all day and they were in the shade, under the trees.

"I just talked to Gus about this," David muttered as he kicked the propeller back into motion. The boat lurched forward, and they moved toward the dock. Candice could see the person glance their way then hurry their pace, disappearing down the driveway between the trees.

"You think it's that groundskeeper again?" Moira called over the noise of the boat.

"I'm almost certain it is," David said. "I'll call Gus and make a complaint when I get back." He frowned. "I might have to go into town to do it, actually. I keep forgetting I don't have any service out here."

He cut the engine as they neared the dock and Eli helped tie the boat down. David was already climbing out, and Moira began gathering up their things. Candice paused to help her husband lift the bucket with the fish out of the boat and place it on the dock before turning back to make sure she hadn't forgotten anything. By the time she was able to focus her attention back on the intruder, David was already heading toward the driveway and the person was nowhere in sight.

She had only gone a couple of steps in his direction

when he paused, and it took a second for her to realize why. Then she heard the sound of a car coming up the driveway, and a moment later, a beat up old pickup truck appeared, slowing down and stopping right in front of David. Candice hurried toward him, eager to know what was going on, and she could hear the others right behind her.

"Glad I got the right place," a familiar female voice said. She was almost certain it was Eden, from the grocery store.

"What's going on?" David asked. "What are you doing here?"

"One of you left your wallet at the store," she said. Candice was close enough now to see through the passenger side window. The woman had rolled it down and leaned awkwardly, holding a wallet out to David. "Thought I'd return it to you – I know phone service can be spotty out here."

"That's mine," Eli said, patting his pockets. "I hadn't even realized it was gone."

David took and handed it back to Eli. He was still frowning at the woman.

"How did you know where we're staying?"

"It's a small town, hon," Eden with a chuckle. "All it took was asking Gus. You have a lovely day now, okay?"

She rolled up the window before David could say anything else and began backing out of the driveway. Candice watched her stepfather frown, then head for the cottage. Candice waved at Eden, then turned to follow him, her mother beside her. Eli was still looking through his wallet, likely making sure nothing was missing.

"What's going on?" Moira asked, sounding irritated. "Why were you so rude to her?"

"Someone was just snooping around our house," David said. "Then, seconds after that person walks down the driveway, Eden appears driving up it. I'm guessing she was the one in here. And I don't like how Gus told her where we were staying without even trying to contact us first."

"It's a tiny town," Moira pointed out. "She found Eli's wallet. He probably didn't see any harm in it."

"Well, whether he saw the problem or not, someone

was snooping around here. Look, the cottage door is still open. And I know Candice saw the same thing I did; someone was in here."

"I did," she confirmed.

"We should go see if anything is missing," David said. "Then I'm going to go to town and call Gus to see what sort of business he's running here. Do you mind if I borrow your phone, Candice?"

She shook her head, more puzzled and worried than anything. She didn't like the fact that someone had been in the cottage without their knowledge, but she also didn't quite understand why her stepfather seemed so on edge.

CHAPTER 8

THEY ATE LUNCH AN HOUR LATER, enjoying the freshly fried fish Eli had caught, and some roasted vegetables her mother had bought. Candice had whipped up some brownies from a mix, but they were still in the oven. The old, gas appliances made her miss her updated, modern kitchen back in the candy shop, and she felt a pang of homesickness – which was ridiculous, since she hadn't even been gone for that long, anyway.

David's tension was still palpable, but while Candice couldn't say she liked the fact that someone had been in their cottage while they were gone, she wondered if he wasn't overreacting. After all, she could think of plenty of reasons why their landlord or the groundskeeper would need to get in when they weren't there, and none of their things seemed to be missing.

At least, until David came into the living room around dinnertime and said, "I can't find my phone."

"Where did you see it last?" Moira asked, looking up from where she was putting away the Monopoly board. The game had lasted for hours and had left Eli the winner. Candice was still shooting him glares occasionally. She could swear he had been cheating, even though he promised he hadn't been. Monopoly was not a game played casually in her family.

"I thought I left it on the nightstand, plugged in," he said. "The battery drains so quickly when it's constantly searching for service. I was going to go into town for service and check an old email from Lenny, but it's gone."

"Have you checked your jacket? Or your pants pockets?"

"I checked everywhere," he said.

"Have you checked the boat?"

He grumbled but admitted he hadn't. He went outside

and returned a couple minutes later, looking even more irritated. "It's not in the boat, and before you ask, it's not in the car either. Whoever was here earlier must've taken it."

"Why would they take your phone?" Moira asked. "My purse was sitting on the kitchen counter the whole time, and I still have all of my cash in my wallet. If someone came here to rob us while we were out on the lake, they would've taken that instead. You probably just put it somewhere weird and forgot where."

"Well, even if that's the case, how am I going to find it?" he asked. "It's not like I can ask one of you to call it – none of our phones even have service out here."

"I'll help you look for it," she said. "You don't need to bite all of our heads off."

"I didn't mean to, but no one else seems to care that a complete stranger broke into the cottage while we were gone, and that the groundskeeper was poking around here last night. All I wanted was a nice family vacation. I can't help but feel that this entire town is somehow acting against us."

"We *are* having a nice vacation," Moira said. "None

of us is comfortable with the fact that someone was in the cottage, but since nothing is missing, I don't think any of us are dwelling on it too much. You're going to talk to Gus tomorrow, anyway. I'm sure it was him; he probably just had to check on something."

David took a deep breath, sighing. "Look, I'm sorry, all right? I just want to find my phone. I'm stressed because of this case with Lenny too. Everything was going smoothly, then I left, and all of a sudden, things just start going wrong. I can't even keep in contact with him since this place has no phone service."

The three of them helped him search for his phone, and while his complaining eventually faded, Candice could see it in his eyes when the phone didn't turn up anywhere; he was convinced that someone had taken it. And honestly, she was beginning to suspect that as well. It didn't make any sense, but they had turned over every cushion in the house and had searched everywhere the phone could possibly be.

Even with the tension over the missing phone and the unexpected guest, the evening was pleasant and Candice woke up well rested the next morning. She, Eli, and David decided to go to town, since Moira said she wanted to stay behind and get some sun and read. Candice and Eli both wanted to explore a bit. David needed to make a couple of calls using Candice's phone, so he dropped them off at the general store, and she handed him her phone after they promised to meet up again in two hours.

Candice knew he was worried about more than just his missing phone, but she couldn't bring herself to ask about it. She wanted to enjoy the vacation. She also knew that she wouldn't be able to help him with anything; he didn't work many cases for his private investigating agency anymore, but when he did, they were usually the more important ones. Even if it was something that he was able to talk about without breaching his client's privacy, he would talk about it with her mom, not with her. She was more than happy to let him borrow her phone, but after that, she removed the matter from her mind. She was here in a lovely little Northern Michigan town with her husband and had two hours in which to walk around and explore the place – as well as pick up some souvenirs for the people who were waiting back home.

She and Eli decided which direction to head down Main Street by flipping a coin, and then started on their way, taking the time to pause and look into stores. They stopped at a couple of secondhand stores; in Candice's experience, they usually had the most interesting things. In the second one, they found a lovely working pocket watch that Eli just had to get for his grandfather.

The next door they passed by was a small candy shop, and they didn't even have to trade a look before they walked inside. Candice stepped into the cool interior and inhaled deeply, relaxing. The building smelled like cotton candy and something fruity, and she saw a taffy puller in front of the window. It was larger than hers and seemed to work better. There was an elderly man behind the counter, and he greeted them cheerfully before turning his attention back to the newspaper he was reading.

Eli wandered off to look at the shelves, but Candice stayed right where she was, looking around. The store was darker than hers, and older. Most of the products were stored in glass jars, and it had a similar cluttered look as the general store, though it wasn't quite as bad. She took a slow walk around the store and enjoyed identifying some of the older types of candy, though this candy shop didn't seem to make as much of its own candy as she did at her store. At last, she picked out some flavored licorice and walked up to the counter to buy it. The old man put his paper down and rang her up.

"You're new to town, aren't you?" he asked as he put the candy in a paper bag.

"Yes," she said, chuckling. "How could you tell? I feel like it's so obvious somehow, but not every single person in town can know literally everyone else."

"Oh, just how you were looking around. Most people have been coming to this store since they were a third of your age. You were looking around like you were a kid in the candy shop for the first time, pardon the pun."

"Oh, I actually own my own candy store, down in the Lower Peninsula. I love looking around other people's shops."

"Really?" he asked, his white eyebrows rising. "That explains why you were examining my taffy puller so closely."

"I've got a smaller model," she said. "It's had some issues, and I've been thinking of replacing it – after I get the air-conditioning replaced, of course. Here, I've actually got a business card with me…" She dug into her purse and opened her wallet, taking one out and handing it over. "If you want to look online, you can see a lot of what we have. We make a lot of our products in-house. I always like talking shop with people who are in the business."

"I'll have to give it a look when I get home," he said. "You're welcome to come in and look around anytime. We've been here for almost eighty years. If you've got any questions, I'm happy to answer them."

"Eighty years," she breathed. She couldn't imagine what her shop would be like all those decades down the road. Would it even still exist? "I might come back in later. Right now, we'd better get going. My husband wanted to check out a few more places, and I know once I start taking talking about candy, I can't stop."

She promised to visit again, then followed Eli out of the shop, glancing back. She loved places like that little, old candy shop, but she knew it would still be there later in the week if she wanted to return.

They reached the end of the business section of Main Street and crossed the road, heading back the other way. They were about to step into a coffee shop when

Candice put her hand on Eli's arm, keeping her eyes on the figure ahead of them that had gotten her attention.

"What is it?" Eli asked.

"Shh," she hushed, keeping her voice low. "Does that guy look familiar to you?"

He looked ahead, following the direction of her nod. "The guy with the brown shirt? No."

Of course not. He hadn't been in the store the day before they left. "I swear I saw him at the candy shop the other day."

"Well, it is almost summer. People travel a lot. Do you want to go say something to him, see if it's the same person?"

"No," she said, frowning. "I'm probably just imagining things. I guess David's got me more on edge than I thought."

"What's with him, anyway?"

"I think it's that case he's working on." They turned, heading into the coffee shop. She wanted something cold and filled with caffeine to drink. "He doesn't want to cut the vacation short, but I think he wants to go back and help Lenny. The fact that he can't call whenever he wants is probably frustrating."

"Plus, he's missing his phone," Eli said.

She grimaced. "Yeah. I feel bad that we didn't find it."

"We tried," he said. "I'm sure it will turn up, eventually. We'll definitely find it before we go home."

"I hope so," she said. The conversation trailed off when they turned to place their orders. Candice ordered an iced caramel macchiato and accepted it from the barista gratefully a minute later, sipping at it as she and Eli stepped back out onto the sidewalk. They still had the rest of the street to finish exploring, then they had to go meet David for their ride home.

He was already parked and waiting for them by the time they got back. He handed her phone over as she got into the car.

"How did it go?" she asked.

"I called Lenny. He's still working the case. No updates, unfortunately. Jeremy is still missing, and our leads on the old missing person case he hired us for have dried up. I talked to Gus too. He said that he did stop by the cottage yesterday, though the timeline doesn't add up – he said he came by just as we were leaving with the boat. He tried to get our attention, but he couldn't. He had to go in to replace the batteries in a fire alarm, and he said he decided to just go ahead and do it when he realized we were all gone. He swears he shut the door afterward, and he would've been gone by the time we got back."

"So, either he's lying, or someone else was snooping around," Candice said, frowning.

"It could've been Eden," Eli pointed out. "Maybe she came to return my wallet and went inside to try to find us."

"Maybe," David said. "I still don't like it."

"I don't think there's anything we can do about it," Candice said. "Let's just go back. Mom will be waiting, and it's almost time for lunch. Plus, it's really nice out today – I might go for a swim."

CHAPTER 9

SEVERAL HOURS LATER, Candice kicked her way over to the dock and hauled herself out of the water, pulling the inner tube up after her. Keeping herself from floating away had been as simple as tying a rope from one of the handles on the tube to the dock, and she had spent a relaxing couple of hours dozing. She had the bad feeling that her sunscreen had worn off, however, and that she was going to be burned the next day, even though she'd spent part of the time in the shade.

The gradually falling evening was beginning to turn the day's warmth chilly, and she was glad to get inside, dry off, and change into warm clothes. Eli

PATTI BENNING

found her while she was brushing her hair and sat down on the bed next to her.

"Do you want to go out tonight?" he asked. "Just the two of us? Not that I don't like being here with your parents, but…"

"I know," she said, smiling at him. "I want to spend some time just the two of us as well. I'm sure they'd like their privacy too. I'll make sure it's okay with Mom if we take the car, then yeah, we can head out."

They traded a quick kiss and she finished with her hair, before getting up to go find her mother, who was quick to agree to them taking her SUV out for the evening. She felt a moment's unease when she realized that meant that her mother and David would be stuck at the cottage with no phone service and no way to get into town, but she reassured herself that it would just be for a couple of hours. Besides, if anything happened, they could go to the groundskeeper's cottage – he had said multiple times to come find him if they needed anything.

The drive to town was quick, and they pulled over in a parking lot for Candice to pull up a list of the local restaurants. They settled on one that looked like a slightly upscale burger joint and drove the short distance to find it. She was thrilled to see that it had an outdoor patio. The lights were just coming on as they parked, and a handful of people were already eating at the tables.

They were seated almost immediately and relaxed at a lovely little table outdoors. Trees bordered one side of the property, and the hum of insects along with the slight smell of smoke from the tiki torches made her smile. This was what she had envisioned her vacation being like.

The waitress brought their menus and took their drink orders, while Candice perused the options, her eyes eventually landing on a Mexican-themed avocado burger that she just had to have. Eli ordered a fried chicken sandwich, and they decided to split a large order of fries.

The service was fast, and it wasn't long before their baskets of food were brought out. Candice took a picture of the burger to show her mother – they both had a love of well-presented food – and dug in, dipping the fries into the smoky, creamy sauce that was served on the side.

"Okay, is it just me, or are these the best burgers ever?" she asked after a few minutes.

"Well, I didn't get a burger so I can't say I have a vote on that, but this chicken is pretty good. Now, the fries…"

"Oh, yes," she said. "The fries are perfect." They were; crispy and flavorful, with enough weight that she could really bite into them.

The waitress approached again, and Candice looked up to ask her to relay their praise to the chef, but the woman was leading another two patrons to the table next to them. She immediately recognized one as Eden, and the other was a woman a few years older than Candice, who looked a lot like Eden; enough that Candice thought she must be her daughter. Eden recognized them right away and waved, but waited until the waitress had taken their orders – they didn't even need to look at the menu to know what they wanted – before walking over to their table.

"Oh, I'm so glad you found this place," she said. "I was going to recommend it to you, but it just slipped my mind. They've got the best burgers this side of the bridge."

"I might have been skeptical if you told me that before I started eating, but you're right," Candice said. "This is great."

"I take it this is a popular place then?" Eli asked.

Eden nodded. "Oh, very much so. We don't have much of a variety up here, but don't people always say it's quality over quantity? Because we've got that in spades. Now, if you'll excuse me, I've got to run to the ladies' room. I'll leave you in peace when I get back, don't worry. You're here to enjoy your vacation, not talk to an old lady like me."

She waved off their denial as she walked away. The woman she was with gave them a slightly embarrassed smile from her table.

"My mother," she said. "I'm visiting her for a couple weeks. I thought I was done being embarrassed by her after high school. I guess I was wrong."

"She's just being friendly," Candice said, smiling. "We really don't mind. It's been... a weird vacation. Friendly faces are nice to see around."

"Where are you guys staying?" the woman asked. "Oh, my name is Missy, by the way."

PATTI BENNING

"I'm Candice," Candice said. Eli introduced himself, then answered the woman's question.

"We have a cottage by the lake."

"Ah," Missy said, as if something suddenly made sense to her. "You're the people staying in number five, aren't you?"

"We are," Eli said. "How did you know?"

"My mother's obsessed with that place. She almost bought it a couple years ago, but Gus snatched it out from under her. She keeps waiting for him to decide the thing is more trouble than it's worth, but it's one of the more popular cottages, so I think she's got her hopes up for nothing. I guess her parents used to own it back before I was born or something."

Candice frowned, filing the information away to tell David later. Maybe he was right and there was something else going on here.

"Well, I don't blame her for liking it. It's a nice place."

"Yeah, but I could do without that creepy groundskeeper," Missy said, shuddering. "We used to rent the place for a week every year back before I moved away. He was always coming around and bothering us. I think he had a bit of a thing for my mom, but I haven't seen him for a while. For all I know, he doesn't work there anymore."

"Is his name Alfie?" Eli asked.

Missy nodded. "I guess he does still work there, then. Anyway, I'm kind of glad she didn't buy it. I'm trying to convince her to move closer to me, actually. It's probably a long shot, since she loves this town so much, and she has the store and everything, but it would be nice to see more of her, and we can't move due to my fiancé's work."

"My mom and I live in different towns, but they're only about ten minutes apart," Candice said. "I've got to say, I'm glad. I would hate only being able to see her a couple times a year."

"Yeah." Missy frowned at her drink. "I hope she's happy here, if she decides to stay. I just wish she'd stop living in the past so much. This town isn't good for that; I don't think a thing has changed since my childhood."

Eden came back a short while later and, after chatting

with Candice and Eli for a few more minutes, turned her attention to her meal with her daughter, while Candice and Eli finished their food. They paid and left, heading back to the SUV together. Candice was eager to return; she had a feeling that David would be interested in knowing what she had found out tonight.

CHAPTER 10

AFTER CANDICE TOLD David about Eden's obsession with their cottage, he seemed even more convinced that someone had been sneaking around the place. Some of David's tension seemed to bleed over to the rest of them and they were on edge the next day, but when nothing strange happened and they didn't have any unexpected visitors, they all managed to relax a bit.

Candice was glad. It was nice to just spend time with her family. Eli and David were having more bonding time as well; the two of them took the boat out again on Thursday to go fishing and came back with a couple more fish for lunch, while she and her mother spent the time talking and baking fresh banana bread.

They hadn't used the fire pit since the first night there, so they decided to make hamburgers on it that evening. This time, they gathered the kindling while it was still light out, and set up a couple of the cheap tiki torches, that promised to keep bugs away, they had bought in town before returning inside to prepare the food. David worked on the hamburger meat while Eli prepared a salad, and Candice and Moira divided their time between the potato salad and a batch of cookies they were making for dessert. They only had a couple of nights left, and they wanted to use up all the food they had bought, so they didn't have to worry about taking it home.

David was just about to go outside to start the fire when someone knocked on the door. All of them traded a glance, then David went to answer it. Candice couldn't see out the door from where she was standing, but she could see her stepfather's face as he frowned and looked around.

"Hello?"

"Who is it?" Moira asked.

"No one's there," David said. He began shutting the door, then froze, his eyes fixed on something on the ground. Curious now, Candice washed her hands off quickly and dried them on a towel before walking over to where he stood.

When she saw what he was looking at, she froze too, feeling the hair on the back of her neck rise. Sitting on the ground just in front of the porch was David's cell phone.

"It couldn't have been there the whole time," she said.

Her mother and Eli approached, and her husband was the first of the two to speak. "Maybe someone found it and put it there."

"Maybe..." David frowned, looking into the darkness. "Why would they knock and then leave, though?"

"Maybe they didn't want to bother us?" Moira suggested, though Candice could tell that her mother didn't really believe that.

His frown deepened, and he stepped outside and crouched down to pick up the phone, pausing to look around. A stick cracked somewhere in the darkness, and he straightened up suddenly.

"Is someone out there?" he called out.

There was no answer, not that Candice had been expecting one. When David began to move further away from the door, Moira stepped outside and grabbed his arm, holding him back.

"Don't go out there alone, David," she said. "I know you've seen most of the same horror movies I have. Splitting up in the dark is never a good idea."

"If someone's out there messing with us –"

"Then they probably want to lure us out for some reason. Going out there alone is just a bad idea. Hold on, I'm going to get my shoes on, and I'll join you."

"I'm coming too," Eli said, already reaching for the shoes that he had left next to the door.

Candice sighed, not wanting to go look for whoever was out there, but she also really didn't want to be left alone. "Me too."

David managed to scrounge up a few flashlights while they were getting their shoes on and handed them out. "Stick together," he said. "Your mom's got the right idea."

Candice didn't need to be told twice. She kept close to her husband, following behind David and her mother.

They all turned their lights on and looked around, but the yard seemed to be empty.

"Hey, what's this?" Eli said. He was standing near the SUV, his light aimed at the windshield.

Candice hurried over, her parents close behind her. She spotted a folded piece of paper under one of the windshield wipers. Carefully, she took it and unfolded it. A handwritten note was scrawled across it, and she squinted her eyes to read it in the unsteady light of the flashlights.

I've been watching you all week. If you want your family to live, come out to the woods alone.

Frowning, and with a coil of fear beginning to unroll in her belly, she handed the note to David. Even in the unsteady light, she could see him go pale.

"We need to get inside, now," he said.

As if waiting for his words, their cottage door slammed shut. All four of them spun to look at it, just as the lights in the kitchen flickered out and the house went dark. David ran back toward the door and tried to open it, but it was locked.

"Do you have your keys?" Moira asked. David shook his head.

"They're inside. "

"So are ours," Candice said.

They shifted to stand closer to each other on the porch, none of them able to keep from glancing around and shifting nervously at the slightest noise.

"What's going on, David?" her mother asked.

"I think it has something to do with the case I'm on with Lenny," he said, shining his flashlight to read the note again. "Whoever I'm looking for, they must be here."

"I think it's time you told us about that case," her mother said.

He nodded reluctantly. "I was hired by a man who is looking for his wife; his name is Jeremy Edwards. His wife went missing last year, but he thinks the police are going in the wrong direction with the case, so he wanted me to find her myself. The police have reason to believe that she was killed, and I have no reason to doubt them, so it's essentially just looking for where she was buried and who might have killed her. Lenny's been doing most of the tracking, I've just been walking him through a couple of things and reaching out to some contacts. This is a lot bigger than most of our cases. I know both of them traveled up north a lot, but they don't have any specific ties to this town that I'm aware of. Still, the killer must be here. They must've gotten wind of this somehow."

"I mentioned to Eden that you were a private investigator," Candice blurted out, horrified. "It was on the first day, before that man died. We had just gotten here."

"Eden went to the bathroom right after that, and minutes later, Frank was dead," Eli said.

Candice's eyes widened. "You don't think that she had something to do with that? If she thought that Frank was David, she might've thought that killing him would make the trail go cold."

The four of them traded horrified looks. It all seemed to make sense.

Light splashed across the house, and Candice heard the sound of a car coming up the driveway. As one, they turned to see a pair of headlights shining at them from the dark. Candice edged closer to the others, unsure whether this was a good sign or not.

"Let's go see what this is all about," David said. "Maybe whoever this is will actually have a working cell phone, for once."

CHAPTER 11

A CAR DOOR SLAMMED, but the headlights were too bright for Candice to see past them. A moment later, a shadowy figure stepped in front of the vehicle.

"Everything all right out here?" a voice rang out. Candice relaxed slightly. It sounded like Gus.

"No, it's not," David said angrily. "Someone's been here. They stole my phone, left a threatening note, and now I think someone's in our cottage. The door slammed shut and someone turned off the lights and locked the door — I can guarantee it wasn't any of us."

"It's probably just the wind," Gus said. "But I'll check it out if you like."

They followed him back to the house and were about to step onto the porch when Moira paused. "Wait, what are you doing here?"

He took out his key ring and began sorting through it as he answered. "Got a call from Alfie," he said. "Said he saw someone suspicious sneaking around again. You're the last people I checked on."

"You don't sound very worried," her mother said.

"Come on, it's Bandon," he said, chuckling. "Nothing bad ever happens around here."

"How well do you know Eden?" David asked suddenly. "The woman who works at the general store."

Looking surprised at the sudden change in topic, Gus paused. "Eden? I've known her as long as I can remember. Why?"

"What do you think of her?"

"She's great," Gus said, finally turning back to the door. "She holds the town together. When she left, last year, I thought people were going to riot. The guy she hired to take care of the store didn't do anything right. When she came back, we were all relieved."

"Where did she go?"

"I don't know if it's any of your business," Gus said, shrugging. "She hasn't made it a secret around here, though. She had a cancer scare and left for treatment. We were all glad when she came back with a clean bill of health." He unlocked the door and pushed it open. "There you go. Do you want me to take a look around the cottage with you? Make sure nothing's hiding in your closets or up the chimney?"

"Yes, please," Moira said firmly when it looked like David was about to turn him down.

Candice was grateful the cottage wasn't very big, because it didn't take them very long to thoroughly search it. Nothing seemed out of place until they reached the bedroom she and Eli shared. The window was open, and the screen was missing from it.

Gus frowned at that. "Has that been missing the whole time? I really should get that replaced. The mosquitos can be brutal."

"No," Candice said, her eyes wide. "It definitely hasn't been. We've been sleeping with it open. Trust me, I would've noticed."

PATTI BENNING

"Well then, what's going on?" Gus asked. He walked out of the room and left the cottage. They all followed him, and she reached out to take Eli's hand. She had no idea what was going on, but she was beyond creeped out.

"It looks like it fell out," Gus said when he reached the back of the building. He nudged the screen on the ground with his boot. "I'll get this set back in for you guys, then I'll head out and leave you to your evening."

It didn't take him long to set the screen back in place. Candice and Eli stayed in the room with him while he did it. Her mother and David continued their discussion in the other room. At last, he pressed on the screen to make sure it wasn't about to budge, then straightened up.

"I'm heading out. You four have a good night, now."

"Thanks for coming out," Moira said, looking up from the couch where she and David were talking. "We'll see you later."

He left the cottage, closing the door behind him. Candice and Eli perched on the couch alongside Moira.

"What's going on?" Candice asked.

"I don't know," David said. "I think we should get out of here. I don't like this, not at all. I know someone was in here. Gus is acting too casual about all of this. We don't have any cell phone service, so I think we need to get to town and call Lenny to see if we can figure out who's behind this, then maybe call the police, depending on what he can tell us."

"All right," Candice said. "I'm going to start packing."

"Don't take everything," Moira said. "Just the important stuff. We can always come back for the rest later. I don't know what's going on either, but your stepfather is worried and that's scaring me more than anything."

"All right," Candice said. She rose and turned toward the bedroom, but the cottage door opened again before she could take more than a step. They all turned to see Gus standing in the doorway, his arms crossed.

"All right, what's the meaning of all this?"

"I have no idea what you're talking about," David said. "Did you see someone in the woods?"

"No," Gus bit out. "My tires are slashed. All four of them. Is this some sort of joke?"

"No," Moira said, holding her hands up. "Why on earth would we do that?"

"I don't know, but the four of you have been nothing but trouble since you got here. No one else has been complaining about mysterious people or missing phones. I don't appreciate it."

"It wasn't us," David said. "Like we told you, there was somebody here earlier."

Gus frowned. "Are you sure? I thought you were just getting spooked. It's a pretty secluded area, some people get uncomfortable."

"Seriously, someone was here," Candice said. "We all live rurally. We aren't jumpy city folk."

"We should go call the police," Gus said. "I think I can move my truck out of the way. Get yours started. We'll go to Alfie's house. He has a land line."

CHAPTER 12

THEIR PLAN WAS SHORT-LIVED. While Gus went to move his car, the rest of them approached Moira's SUV. David had the keys in his hand and hit the button to unlock the vehicle, causing the lights to flash. Eli froze, his hand catching Candice's wrist.

"Look at the tires," he said. They were flat.

"Go back inside," David said quickly. He turned, waving at Gus, trying to catch the man's attention. Gus honked his horn, and Candice turned toward the house, confident that the other man at least knew that something was wrong. Then he flashed his lights. Twice.

She turned, frowning, about to ask David what on earth the other man was trying to say, when a hand fastened around her wrist and pulled her to the side and against a warm body. She cut off her scream when she realized it was just Eli.

"What are you doing?" she hissed. His grip tightened on her, but he didn't answer. She realized he was staring off into the darkness, at a spot that would have been right behind her before he pulled her away.

She followed his gaze and almost screamed again when she saw the dark, bulky, misshapen outline of something standing just beyond the range of the head-lights. Her mother noticed her jolt of fear and turned around as well.

"David!" she shouted, pointing. David spun around, the beam of his flashlight cutting through the dark-ness and lighting up the figure.

It wasn't a person, but rather, two people. Alfie was holding a man in a brown shirt by the arm, and neither of them looked pleased.

"Sorry for scarin' yeh," he said. Candice wanted to add "again," but refrained from it, knowing that it was her fear making her snappy. "But I caught this guy sneaking around when I came over to check on you."

A car door slammed, distracting them all for an instant, and Gus rushed over. "Alfie, it's just you. You almost gave me a heart attack. These people have got me spooked." He paused. "Who is that?"

"I don't know," Alfie said. "I saw him poking around, and I thought he looked like he was up to no good."

The man he was holding onto struggled, raising his face to glare at the groundskeeper, and David called out, "Hey, I know him. Let him go, he's a client of mine."

Looking puzzled, Alfie let the man go. Now that he was standing up straight and facing them, Candice recognized him as the man who stopped in at the candy shop the day before they left — the same man she thought she'd seen in Bandon earlier in the week. Jeremy. He shot one last glare at the groundskeeper, then shifted his attention to David.

"What are you doing here?" David asked.

"I – I needed to talk to you," Jeremy said. "I couldn't reach you on the phone."

"How did you even know where we were?"

"Lenny told me," Jeremy said.

David sighed. "All right. Let's go in and talk."

"David, can't it wait?" Moira asked.

"Look, Jeremy might be able to help me figure out who's doing all this," David said. With a sigh, Moira crossed her arms. David and Jeremy headed toward the cottage, David waving at them to follow.

"Wait, what am I supposed to do about my truck?" Gus called out.

"I can go back to my house and call a wrecker out," Alfie said. "It will only take me a few minutes, so hold tight. I'll come back when I'm done."

He walked away. With a sigh and a glance at her husband, who was halfway to the cottage and waiting impatiently, Moira said, "Let's go in."

Inside the cottage, David and Jeremy sat across from each other in the living room while the rest of them crowded around in the kitchen to give them some privacy while they talked about the case.

"You might as well help yourselves to potato salad,"

Moira said to Gus, who was shooting the bowl a hungry look. "I've got a feeling our dinner's been put on hold indefinitely."

"Thanks," he said, accepting the plate she got out of the cupboard to hand to him. "This looks good."

Candice leaned against the counter next to her mother, eyes darting between Jeremy and David. Something was bothering her. How had Jeremy known exactly where to find them? She didn't think Lenny would have simply told him where to find David. He would have left a message first at the very least, and David had been using her phone to call him every day. Plus, what on earth could Jeremy want to talk about badly enough to drive four hours up north and wander around in the dark woods for who knew how long just to find them? Plus, she was sure she had seen him in town the other day. If he had been here for that long, why hadn't he come to talk to David before? Suddenly, it all clicked. She gasped, then tried to disguise it as a cough when she saw Jeremy's eyes slide over to her.

"Are you okay, sweetie?" her mother asked.

"I'm fine," Candice said. She looked over at Eli, who

was looking at her in concern as well. She tilted her head toward their room and made sure he followed her inside, waiting until the door was shut behind them before speaking.

"It's Jeremy," she said.

"What do you mean?"

"I mean it's him. He's the one behind all this."

"I don't understand. Why would he be doing all this? David's working for him, isn't he?"

"I don't know, but it makes sense. I told him where we were going the day before we left. And remember the other day when we were walking around town? I swear I saw him. He probably asked Eden what cottage we were staying at, or maybe he just overheard it – no, actually, I don't think he even knew where we were exactly. Remember, the first night we were here someone was poking around, and Alfie said that they'd been to a couple cottages. He was probably looking in windows until he found the right one. It's him, Eli. I just know it."

"Well, what do we do?" he asked.

"I don't know. Just wait and hope he leaves soon?"

"Candice, if he's really the one behind all of this, I don't think he's leaving. He must've come out here for a reason, and he didn't slash all of our tires and leave a note on the windshield just to sit down and talk with David. If he wanted to do that, he could knock on the door."

"You're right." She felt her heart begin to pound. Jeremy wasn't there for an innocent reason. Her parents could be in danger as they spoke. She yanked open the bedroom door and hurried out into the living room, then froze, not sure what to do.

"Is everything okay?" David asked, looking at her.

"I – I'm fine," Candice said.

She saw a frown cross Jeremy's face for a fraction of a second, then he stood up.

"Well, I'd better be going," he said.

"We haven't even resolved anything," David said, sounding annoyed. "Just sit back down. You chased me all the way out here, the least you can do is help us figure out who's threatening my family. The person responsible for your wife's disappearance has to be someone in this town. Just walk me through the last few weeks before her disappearance again."

"No, no, I should get going. I've already intruded enough. I'll see myself out."

"I really need to get to the bottom of all this. My family might be in danger. Can we at least talk while you walk to your car?"

"All right," Jeremy said, practically jumping out of his seat. "Come on."

Candice took a step forward, but Eli put a hand on her arm. She looked at him and saw the silent plea in his eyes for her not to endanger herself, but David was her stepfather — and in many ways, more of a father than her actual father ever was. She couldn't let him put himself in danger.

Jeremy reached the front door and pulled it open, and Candice took another step forward. "David, no!" she called out. "He's the one behind all of this!"

David froze, but Jeremy almost seemed to be expecting her words. He reached into his pocket and in a smooth motion withdrew a sharp looking knife, slashing it at her stepfather. David jumped back and managed to deflect the man's hand, backpedaling so quickly that he almost tripped.

"Hey!" Gus put the plate of potato salad down and moved toward Jeremy, who backed up, pushing the screen door open behind him and holding the knife at the ready.

"I'll kill anyone who comes close," he said.

"What's going on?" David asked. "Jeremy, what are you —" He broke off, his eyes widening slightly. "You killed her, didn't you? Your wife. And... did you kill Frank too? That man who looked like me?"

"I hired you because the police were closing in on me," Jeremy said. "I thought if I gave you the right sort of wrong information, you'd be able to make it look like she just left the country or something. But Lenny kept calling me and asking me all these questions, and he seemed really excited about you being on the right track. I realized that you were going to come to the same conclusion the police were beginning to. I couldn't let that happen! Killing you would at least get the police off my back for a while. It would have given me enough time to leave the country."

"How did you even know where we were going?" David asked.

"It was my fault," Candice said. "I told him. I didn't know who he was when he came into the candy shop, and I told him we were going to Bandon."

"Your daughter got lucky that day," Jeremy said. "I was going to kidnap her and use her to make you drop the case. But then she mentioned you were all going up north, and I figured it would be the perfect time to get you on your own. All I knew was that whatever I did to stop you, it couldn't point back to me."

Gus moved toward him again, and Jeremy twitched, pointing the knife at him. When David shifted, he seemed torn, looking back and forth between the two men.

"Just put the knife down," David said. "We can talk about this. You just want all of this to be over, right? Don't hurt any of us, and you can walk away."

"Shut up," Jeremy said. "I just need time to think –"

He broke off as a pair strong arms wrapped around him from behind, pinning the hand that was holding the knife to his body. He struggled, trying to break free, but Alfie held him tighter, his years of chopping wood and doing odd jobs outdoors giving him the upper body strength he needed to keep Jeremy restrained.

"I knew this guy was up to no good," he said. "Do any of you have zip ties? I'm going to have to run back home and make another call, this time to the police."

EPILOGUE

"I GOT THIS FOR YOU." Candice held out the small package wrapped in brown paper. Allison gave an excited squeal as she took it.

"I love souvenirs!" She unwrapped it, revealing a bronze pin Candice had found at the antique store her second time through that read, *Bandon; You'll never forget us!*

"I have something else for you, but it's in the fridge and it's for everyone."

"Really?" Allison asked, half distracted as she attached the pin to her apron, where it joined the others. She grinned up at Candice. "What do you think?"

"It looks great."

"Thanks! Now, what's this about a surprise in the fridge?"

Candice led her friend into the candy shop's kitchen, where she made a beeline for the refrigerator and pulled the door open, revealing a boxed up rhubarb pie, which she had bought when they stopped at the general store on their way out of town.

"Bandon has a lot of claims to fame, but I think the pies really are some of the best I've tasted."

"Now I've got to try it."

Candice cut herself a piece once Allison had hers, and the two of them sat on stools in the kitchen. Candice took a bite of hers and closed her eyes, sighing. She really wished she had grabbed a second one for herself.

"Right, I've got a lot to tell you about the trip."

"Lay it on me," Allison said. "Don't make me talk too much though. Gotta focus on my pie."

Candice started, and by the time she was done, the pie

LEMON TWISTS AND TURMOIL

was sitting on the counter, forgotten, while her best friend stared at her, her mouth hanging open.

"So, the creepy groundskeeper actually saved your life?"

"Well, it was one against four, so I don't think Jeremy would have actually managed to hurt any of us, especially since he wasn't able to get David on his own. But, yeah, he saved the day."

"I guess that Jeremy guy should have thought twice about hiring David's company to try to track down a fake trail for his wife. You'd think he would have heard of David's reputation and would have gone with someone else."

"Well, David doesn't work on most cases anymore, so he probably thought Lenny wouldn't do as good of a job. Lenny's not bad about what he does by any means, but David is scary good at it."

"Then he realized his mistake." Allison shook her head.

"First, he decided to kidnap me. Then when he found out we were all going to spend a week in the middle of nowhere, he decided to try to kill David instead.

He stole David's cell phone and tried to send off a bunch of text messages to make it look like David went crazy, but it never actually worked since he didn't have any service. It was really creepy."

"Your life is crazy, do you know that?" her friend asked, shaking her head.

"Don't remind me," Candice said with a groan. "All I wanted was a nice, relaxing vacation, but it feels like getting back to work will be the vacation from my vacation. One of these days, things are going to calm down and I'll have a nice, boring, regular life."

"Keep telling yourself that," Allison said with a chuckle.

AUTHOR'S NOTE

I'd love to hear your thoughts on my books, the story-lines, and anything else that you'd like to comment on —reader feedback is very important to me. My contact information, along with some other helpful links, is listed on the next page. If you'd like to be on my list of "folks to contact" with updates, release and sales notifications, etc.... just shoot me an email and let me know. Thanks for reading!

Also...

... if you're looking for more great reads, Summer Prescott Books publishes several popular series by outstanding Cozy Mystery authors.

CONTACT SUMMER PRESCOTT BOOKS PUBLISHING

Twitter: @summerprescott1

Bookbub: https://www.bookbub.com/authors/summer-prescott

Blog and Book Catalog: http://summerprescottbooks.com

Email: summer.prescott.cozies@gmail.com

YouTube: https://www.youtube.com/channel/UCngKNUkDdWuQ5k7-Vkfrp6A

And...be sure to check out the Summer Prescott Cozy Mysteries fan page and Summer Prescott Books Publishing Page on Facebook – let's be friends!

To download a free book, and sign up for our fun and exciting newsletter, which will give you opportunities to win prizes and swag, enter contests, and be the first to know about New Releases, click here: http://summerprescottbooks.com

Made in the USA
Middletown, DE
27 September 2021